D0525694

YOU
BE THE
DETECTIVE

Other titles by Marvin Miller include:
You be the Jury
You be the Jury 2
Your own Super Magic Show

Marvin Miller

Illustrated by
Bryan Reading

Hippo Books
Scholastic Children's Books
London

Scholastic Children's Books,
Scholastic Publications Ltd,
7-9 Pratt Street, London NW1 0AE, UK

Scholastic Inc.,
730 Broadway, New York, NY 10003, USA

Scholastic Canada Ltd,
123 Newkirk Road, Richmond Hill,
Ontario, Canada L4C 3G5

Ashton Scholastic Pty Ltd,
P O Box 579, Gosford, New South Wales,
Australia

Ashton Scholastic Ltd,
Private Bag 1, Penrose, Auckland,
New Zealand

First published in the USA by Scholastic Inc., 1991
First published in the UK by
Scholastic Publications Limited, 1992

Text copyright © Marvin Miller, 1991
Illustrations copyright © Bryan Reading, 1992

ISBN 0 590 55003 9

Typeset in Plantin by
Contour Typesetters,
Southall, London
Printed by Cox & Wyman Ltd,
Reading, Berks

For Randy
and Audrey

CONTENTS

Welcome to Your
New Job!

Welcome to Your New Job!

Welcome to the CID. My name is Detective Alexander Riddle. As you know, this is my last day in the job. You will be my replacement.

I have been a detective here for ten years, ever since I left law school. It's a good place to work. Chief Inspector Anvil is a tough but fair boss. But I have decided that being a detective is not what I really want to do in life, so I'm going back to college—to become an artist.

I am giving all my files to you. As you will see, I do my best thinking with a pencil and a drawing pad in my hands. For every case, I have sketched a drawing of the scene of the crime. There are often clues at the scene of a crime that a sharp eye can detect. Take a good look at the drawing and read my report of the case.

At the end of each case you will find another drawing. This drawing shows my sketch that solves the mystery. You will notice that I have cut this drawing into pieces and rearranged the pieces.

I have done this for two reasons.

First, you will have a chance to check my report and come to your own conclusion about the case. Then you can check your solution with mine by cutting out the pieces of the puzzle and putting my drawing back together again. If you can't wait to do the puzzle, you can find my written solution at the end of each case.

Second, Chief Inspector Anvil is a puzzle fan. He loves putting together jigsaw puzzles. When I found this out, I decided always to give him the solutions to my cases as jigsaw puzzles.

Well, I see it's getting late. Gosh, I'm going to miss this place. Here are my files. Good luck! I'm off to be an artist.

You be the detective!

The Case of the Circus Footprints

On 31 August, a worried man rang my office at Headquarters. "The circus has been robbed," he said.

"My name is Richard Riley, and I am the owner of Riley's All-Star Circus," he said. "We have our big top pitched on the Higgins Secondary School football field. Do you know it? This morning a cash box with the wages for my performers was stolen."

Suddenly childhood memories came rushing back to me. I had seen "Robust Richard" Riley doing his circus strongman act on my twelfth birthday. He was the strongest man I had ever seen. It seemed incredible that anyone would dare rob him.

"Last night, we finished the last performance of the summer," Riley continued.

"I counted the money this morning. My cashier also counted. I hid the cash box in the box office. When I returned from breakfast, it had gone."

I was on the scene in fourteen minutes flat.

I could see the bright red and green stripes of the big top from the car park. I

could also see a row of circus caravans parked about twenty yards behind the tent. The field was surrounded by a high wire-mesh fence.

Riley met me at the gate—the only gate. With him was a man in uniform.

"Detective Riddle! I'm so glad you are here," he said. "I'll show you where we had the money hidden."

Riley led me along a short sawdust path to the box office. The sawdust felt like little pillows under my feet. I looked behind me. I made a footprint with every step.

The box office had windows on three sides, including a big window in the door. The door was open, but no glass was broken. Except for a chair, the office was completely empty.

"Do you see the footprints?"

Riley's finger pointed to the side of the box office. About two dozen footprints led from the box office to the caravans. Another row of footprints led from the caravans to the box office. I also saw what looked like two palm prints.

I took out my pad and pencil. I began to draw what I was seeing:

It was clear that these were the footprints of the thief who had walked from the caravans to the box office and back again. Unwittingly the thief had left his footprints in the soft, freshly-swept sawdust. But why were there also two palm prints? Had the thief fallen? Perhaps he had a bad leg.

I looked again at the footprints. They were small. A size five shoe, I guessed. The heel of each shoe had made a small, deep hole. Obviously they were high-heeled shoes. Now I imagined my thief differently. He was a she.

"I read in the newspaper that your cashier is also the ringmaster, or should I say ringmistress, of the circus," I said to Riley.

"Oh, you can't possibly suspect Tara!" he cried. "Miss Blossom is by far the most faithful member of our small circus. I cannot run the show without her," Riley protested. "Besides, she was with me at breakfast this morning."

"Have any of your performers injured their legs lately?" I asked him. I was thinking about the palm prints again.

"We are all fit and well," he said. "I am proud to say that not a single performer has needed to see a doctor all year."

"Did you see anyone else up early this morning?" I asked. "Besides Miss Blossom?"

"Just Mr Wilde, the animal trainer."

"What exactly was he doing?" I asked.

"He was sweeping the grounds. I saw him at about eight o'clock, just as Miss Blossom and I went out of the gate to breakfast."

"Is this unusual for Mr Wilde?"

"Not at all. His animals trample the path after every performance. He sweeps it smooth every morning," Riley said.

Whether or not Wilde had committed the crime, I already owed him a favour. His sweeping had provided me with the time of the crime. The footprints had been made some time after eight o'clock this morning.

"Mr Riley," I said. "Would you please make me a list of the shoe sizes of all your performers?"

Riley gave me a puzzled look. But then he nodded and left.

I examined the footprints again. Then I followed them with my eyes. Where did they lead to? Where did they come from?

They began and ended where the sawdust ended—at the raised wooden platform. That platform connected all of the caravans to one another. All trace of any footprints ended at the platform.

I looked down the long row of caravans. Each caravan had a name on it. *Tara. Richard. Big George Wilde. Alexandra Loftwalker. Button the Clown. Bert Twirl.*

Next to each name was a giant painting of the performer. I already knew who the first three were. Alexandra Loftwalker was a tightrope walker. She was shown balancing on one foot, high above a crowd. Button the Clown was shown with a pie being thrown in his face. Bert Twirl, the acrobat, was doing a handstand.

I had never had a list of suspects so large and brightly painted. I liked it.

"I found these," said a voice.

It was Riley, back again with the list. He was also holding up a pair of high-heeled shoes.

"They were behind the caravans," he said. The shoes were covered with sawdust, inside and out. "They are Tara's, if you must know," he said with a frown. "But she wasn't wearing them this morning. She was wearing her blue trainers. I remember."

"Thank you," I said. "Thank you very much."

Here is the list of shoe sizes Riley gave me:

Tara Blossom (cashier): size 5.

Big George Wilde (animal trainer): size 10.

Alexandra Loftwalker (tightrope walker): size 7½.

Barry Buttonni (Button the Clown): size 8.

Bert Twirl (acrobat): size 9½.

Richard Riley (owner): size 12.

Only Blossom had the right shoe size. But she had been with Riley.

I looked at her shoes. I checked one against the thief's footprints. It fitted perfectly.

It gave me an idea. Perhaps the thief had simply slipped Tara's two small shoes over the toes of his larger shoes. I decided to test the idea on a smooth area of sawdust. I expected to succeed, of course. But after two steps, I fell over. It didn't work.

The thief had needed only one hand to catch himself when he fell. I suppose I didn't have the knack. The new footprints I had made with Tara's shoes looked different from the thief's footprints. I could even see the outline of my own shoe circling the outline of the smaller shoe. Someone with bigger feet couldn't possibly have put on Tara's shoes.

I sat down in disgust.

I looked at Riley's list again. I looked at my sketch. Palm prints. Two palm prints. What could it be? Then I noticed that there was a right-hand palm print going towards the box office, and a left-hand palm print returning from it. Why? I had an idea. I picked up my pencil, then my pad.

I began by drawing the scene of the crime. Then, for fun, on the next six pages, I drew each performer in the middle of his or her circus act. One of the drawings caught my eye.

Suddenly I had it! It was the only way. It made sense and it was easy.

To the criminal's portrait, I added a pair of red shoes and a brown shoulder bag with the money in it. At last, the solution was mine.

On my way out, I stopped at the gate. I told Riley who the thief was.

Then I borrowed a pair of scissors and cut my final drawing into little pieces. I knew that when Chief Inspector Anvil put this puzzle together, he'd go crazy.

FINAL REPORT

It was the palm prints that gave away Bert Twirl. None of the performers' feet could fit into Tara's shoes. But someone's *hands* could easily fit inside.

Only one person could have walked to the ticket booth with his hands in Tara's shoes—an acrobat!

But Bert's hands had slipped out of the shoes—twice. He caught his balance, leaving the palm prints behind.

—CASE CLOSED—

The Case of the Lost Lighthouse Keeper

On 15 July, an unusual call shattered the late-night quiet of Headquarters. "It's a ship-to-shore call," the CID telephonist said. "Who will take it?"

I took the call.

"Hello, Riddle? This is Malcolm Newhouse the Coastguard," barked a crackly voice. "I'm calling from Seagull Strait. A cargo ship, the *Rhonda Sue*, ran aground tonight. What's left of her is hanging off Hopeless Rock. We have a real mess here, and we suspect that something has happened at the Seagull Point lighthouse. Can you help us out there?"

"Newhouse," I said, "why are you calling the CID? Problems with lighthouses are taken care of by the Coastguard."

"We've called out all our crews to help clear up. We can't cover the lighthouse tonight." The hiss of static filled the phone for a moment. Then Newhouse continued, "The captain of the *Rhonda Sue* missed the channel because the light never came on at Seagull Point lighthouse."

A shiver ran down my spine. Seagull Point lighthouse was one of the last non-automatic lighthouses left in the country. Old Man Kettle had run the Seagull Point lighthouse since I was old enough to know what a lighthouse was. It was unthinkable that he would forget to turn it on.

I was on the scene in half an hour.

In the dark, the houses on Seagull Point Road looked eerie among the tall pines. I saw a light on in every house. Everyone was at home.

As I turned left onto Lighthouse Road, the sight of the red and white stripes of the old lighthouse tower gave me a warm feeling inside. Seagull Point lighthouse itself looked as pretty as a postcard. Two small outdoor spotlights on the front lawn lit it up like a museum piece. But without its powerful beam, it looked dead.

I parked and pulled out my bag, a torch,

and my sketch pad from the boot. Then I climbed the stairs to the top room of the tower. I saw no one, but I did spot a large switch. It looked like something from the horror film *Frankenstein*. It was turned to "Off". I quickly dusted for fingerprints. Then, after a moment's hesitation, I turned it on.

The powerful light that filled the round room made me squint. Soon the huge lens in the centre began to revolve.

At least the Coastguard has its light back again, I thought to myself. Satisfied for now, I descended the steep, twisting stairs.

The living quarters downstairs were deathly quiet. Usually the foghorn blared. But tonight, I could hear the waves outside. Old Man Kettle was nowhere to be found. What had happened to him?

Then I saw the note. It was scrawled on a blackboard under the word *Weather*. The note read:

Seagull Point Lighthouse
dark = Kettle safe.

My heart sank. It looked like someone had kidnapped Old Man Kettle. The note on the blackboard seemed to be a warning. It seemed to say that Kettle would be safe only as long as the lighthouse light was turned off.

I thought of the switch I had turned on. Had the kidnappers seen the light go back on? What would they do now?

I searched for the chalk used to write the note. But the house was empty of pens, pencils, or anything else to write with! I was puzzled.

I walked into the kitchen. It looked as if there had been a struggle. Two chairs were knocked over. Sugar had been spread across the table. The floor was wet with spilled coffee. A mug lay on its side on the floor. A bag of sugar was still standing on the table.

The mug had just a trace of coffee left in it. Compared to the air in the room, the mug felt warm. That meant the crime had happened within the hour. The kidnappers were close—close enough to see the lighthouse light.

I sketched the scene. As I worked, the overhead light caught the surface of the table in a new way. There on the table, I could just make out a number drawn in spilled sugar:

But what could "337" possibly stand for? I remembered Kettle. He wasn't stupid. He may have been expecting trouble before it happened. The "337" was probably a clue that Kettle had written as to who his kidnappers were. But what was it? Part of a telephone number? An address?

I called Headquarters. With a few re-inforcements, I rounded up three suspects: Captain Morgan Helm, Bradford T. Shipworthy, and Lee Ron Tillerman. They all lived on Seagull Point Road, within plain view of the lighthouse. As I interviewed them, two of my fellow detectives searched the suspects' houses for Kettle.

All three suspects looked tired and claimed to have been sleeping at the time of the crime. All had known Kettle for years, and claimed to have liked him. But each one had a reason for wanting the Seagull Point light to go off.

A year ago, Morgan Helm had been the captain of the *Rhonda Sue*. Then, after months of poor health, he had lost his shipping licence. A man named Hogshead had taken his job on the *Rhonda Sue*.

Helm admitted that he and Hogshead were enemies. Helm said he had often wished that the *Rhonda Sue* and Hogshead would go down in a storm. But he added that he would never try to make such a thing happen.

Bradford Shipworthy was the owner of the small shipping company that owned the *Rhonda Sue*. Shipworthy's company had been losing money for two years. He said he had become depressed about it. Then a month ago, he took out a large insurance policy that would pay him for accidents at sea. If the *Rhonda Sue* sank, the insurance company would pay him a lot of money. But he said he had had nothing to do with the accident.

Of the three suspects, Lee Ron Tillerman knew Kettle best. By trade, he was a housepainter. He said he had painted the first red stripes on the Seagull Point lighthouse. For fifteen years, Tillerman and Kettle had played draughts together almost every day. But recently they had had an argument. Kettle thought that Tillerman was cheating at draughts, and Tillerman had been angry. Tillerman had called him "a cantankerous landlubber."

"I couldn't put up with his accusations, could I?" Tillerman said.

I asked the three in turn about the "337".

Helm said he thought that the "337" was a code. "Kettle is an amateur cryptographer," he said. "Codes are his hobby."

Shipworthy and Tillerman offered no new ideas. All three also denied having written the note on the blackboard.

After the interviews, I returned to my office with a sketch pad. I had to work fast. Kettle was still in danger.

The clue had to mean something. But what? The phone number idea seemed to lead nowhere. The local numbers all started with 609, not 337. Addresses in the area were only two digits long, not three.

I wrote out a simple code I remembered from school. We had used it to pass notes in the library. *1=A, 2=B, 3=C, 4=D, 5=E, 6=F, 7=G, etc*. I wrote. Using this code, "337" might spell something. But "337" decoded into "CCG". Were those letters initials? None of the suspects had those initials.

If Kettle had known he was in trouble, he would have been clever enough not to hide the meaning of his clue too carefully.

Suddenly I had it. It was simple!

Quickly I redrew the scene of the crime with Kettle sitting at the table. Now Kettle's hasty message was as loud and clear as a bell. I could see the solution clearly.

With one quick phone call I had my kidnapper before me in handcuffs. After hearing my evidence against him, he confessed and promised that the old light-keeper was still within earshot of his beloved lighthouse, and safe.

After the police took the culprit away, I cut up my drawing and put it in the file. I knew that when Chief Inspector Anvil put this puzzle together, the solution would really leap out at him.

FINAL REPORT

Kettle had been sitting on the *other side* of the table. The kidnapper must have been with him.

Kettle suspected trouble. He spilled some sugar while making his coffee. Then he secretly wrote his kidnapper's first name in the sugar—LEE.

Upside down, it looked like the number 337. Lee Ron Tillerman had no idea that this clue would tip off the CID.

—CASE CLOSED—

The Case of the Edible Evidence

On 3 November, I was hanging up my blue parka on the office coatstand when the owner of Frank's Supermarket phoned Headquarters. He sounded upset.

"I had a break-in, Detective Riddle. I think it happened last night."

I hadn't even shaken the snow off my boots. Now I might not have to.

"They didn't steal money. They stole a handful of fruit and vegetables," he went on. "One carrot. Some cherries. And a few figs. That's about all. It's the strangest break-in I've ever seen. Can you come over?"

I decided not to rush, considering the crime Frank had described. But even if it had been more serious, I still wouldn't have had to rus... could be there in two minutes on foot, ... over all those unshovelled pavement...

Frank's ...ermarket is on the same street as CID he...uarters. Four days out of five, I was the...t lunchtime to buy a turkey sandwich ...hy usual tuna on brown bread with lettu...and tomato. I saw more of Frank tha...aw of many of my best friends.

I put m...at back on and grabbed my pad.

When I ...ived on the scene, Frank was waiting fo...e outside. "I haven't opened for busine...et. I just can't tell how serious this is. M:...this weirdo will come back."

I saw ...ing wrong outside. The big glass wind...looked a bit steamed up, but they wer...broken. "Your heating is certainly ...king," I said.

"I ope...this lock myself this morning," Frank sa...He was pointing to a heavy padlock h...ging from a hasp on the opened door. Th...oor was not damaged in any way.

We ste...d inside and stamped our feet to get the...w off our boots. It felt good to get in out...he wind. "So how did the thief get in?" I...ked. "A back door?"

"Yeah. It's over here," Frank said, pointing to a door behind the sandwich counter. The door seemed to open out into an alley.

"No one has ever tried to prise open a door in my shop," Frank said. "But when I came in this morning, the back door was wide open."

"Was the shop this warm when you arrived?"

"Almost," he said. "I've only been here ten minutes. I turned the heating up when I got here."

The crime must have happened this morning, not last night, I thought. The shop would have been freezing if the door had been open to the outside for more than an hour or so.

"I may even have left the door unlocked myself last night," Frank said, shaking his head. "I just don't remember. I was in a rush to drive home before the snow settled. You know, by two o'clock yesterday afternoon they were talking about closing schools today. So I closed up early."

"Do you remember shutting the door?"

"Oh, yes. The door was shut tight when I left," said Frank.

"So let's see what the thief took."

Frank led me down Aisle 1. First he showed me a bag of carrots. The bag was split open at the top. "One carrot is missing from this bag," Frank said. "One. Just one."

"Are you sure?" I asked.

"I buy carrots by the bag. There are seven in each bag. This one has six and a big hole."

He pointed further down the aisle. A bunch of cherries had been spilt across the floor.

"A handful of cherries has gone," Frank explained.

"Were the aisles clear last night before you left?"

"They were clean and clear, as usual. I always check the aisles before I leave," he said. We walked to the back of the shop and turned into Aisle 2.

"A few figs," Frank said, holding up a torn cellophane packet. "Not the whole packet of figs, mind you—just a few. I mean, does that make sense? Whoever it was, he wasn't very hungry."

I had to agree.

I told Frank to check his shop one more time, top to bottom, and to call me if he found anything more valuable missing. I said I would talk to his neighbours, and give him a report as soon as I could.

"Today's tuna—right?" he said as I left.

I smiled. But I felt more puzzled than hungry.

Outside, I talked to two of Frank's neighbours. They stopped shovelling just long enough to say they had seen nothing suspicious.

"Just all these kids out today," said one, ducking a volley of well-packed snowballs.

Nearby, a worker in a yellow helmet climbed down from a nearby telegraph pole to answer questions. He said he had not seen a thing.

I crossed the street. Two kids were making a huge snowball from the snow on the library lawn. A sign in the library window read:

Wind had packed the snow right over the book slot.

Two doors away was Café 24, where I was certain I could find a witness. Café 24 was named after the number of hours it was open each day. Only one other place on the street stayed open as many hours as Café 24 did, and I worked for that place. So I knew Café 24 well.

From two in the morning to ten at night Donna Margonni sits at the till. She would have had a clear view of Frank's at the time of the crime.

"Not much business last night, Detective," she said. "Everyone must have gone home before the snow. It was quiet out there until the first snowploughs came," she said. "Anyway, I suppose I was more interested in watching the snow fall than in what was going on at Frank's."

I asked her to question her late-night customers anyway, when she saw them next. Then I trudged back to Headquarters.

The next day was quiet at work. The snow must have temporarily put a damper on crime. It was sunny out and warm, with no wind. Much of the snow had melted. So I decided to take a stroll to Frank's to see if he had found anything more valuable than cherries missing.

"Nothing," he told me. "In fact, I found an extra two dollars on the counter after you left yesterday."

I ordered a turkey sandwich and a milk shake.

As I left Frank's, I saw Donna in the window at Café 24, so I dropped in again.

Donna's customers had no new leads for me.

"We make better milk shakes than Frank's," she said as I opened the door to leave. "You should know that, Detective Riddle."

On the way back to Headquarters, I passed the library again. Grass was showing through the melted snow. Suddenly I spotted something interesting: a carrot in a small patch of snow. Looking closer, I saw that the wide end of the carrot had been chopped off and was missing.

Less than a yard away, in a pool of water, were eight cherry stones. Nearby lay a few uneaten figs.

The stolen goods—but why here? And why would anyone steal them and only eat the cherries? This little case was beginning to amuse me.

I took out my pad and sketched the scene:

I studied my drawing for a while. Then I made a new drawing. Suddenly I had it.

Frank, Donna and I didn't have a burglar in our street. The thief had merely been caught up in a harmless prank.

I quickly cut up my new drawing and stuck it in my sketch pad. I knew that when Chief Inspector Anvil saw this puzzle, he'd be really surprised. The solution to the crime was as plain as the nose on his face.

FINAL REPORT

This case was a tough one. As I studied my first drawing, I started to think, maybe the robber never meant to eat the carrot or the figs.

I remembered the kids making the giant snowball. Then it hit me. They were making a *snowman!*

It had a carrot for a nose. The figs were used for eyes and buttons. The outline of a mouth was dotted with eight cherry stones. When the kids discovered that Frank had left the back door of the supermarket unlocked, they had helped themselves, leaving the money on the counter to pay for what they'd taken.

If the sun hadn't melted the snowman, this case would have been a lot easier to solve.

—CASE CLOSED—

The Case of the Haunted House

On 31 October, an estate agent rang Headquarters from a call box on Lake Avenue. She sounded out of breath.

"Detective, I need your help." Her voice quavered as she spoke. "I've seen a ghost."

I suggested that she might have the wrong number.

"I don't really think it's a ghost," she continued. "But the gardener at the house thinks it's a ghost, and two different neighbours have seen lights on at night in this house. It's supposed to be empty." The caller identified herself as Allegra Bramble, an agent for True View Properties.

I looked at my watch, then at my calendar. A crime wave was sweeping a neighbourhood on the other side of town. I had no time for investigating Halloween pranks.

"Earl Browning hired me two months ago to sell his family's hundred-year-old country home," Bramble explained. "It's been empty for years. They keep a gardener, so it wouldn't look empty. But I'm certain that it isn't empty any more."

"Miss Bramble," I said. "I have seven burglaries on my hands in the Broadview area. But if you really think your situation deserves my immediate attention, then I'll come straight over."

"I know it does," she said.

Forty minutes later, I drove up the dirt-and-gravel drive of 12 Lake Avenue. I was glad to get out of my car. Lake Avenue curves like a snake along the shore of Glass Lake. Sometimes it feels more like a BMX track than a quiet country road. The lake itself has so many inlets that most of the houses sit on their own private peninsulas. The old Browning house was one of these.

Bramble was leaning against her car.

"I've only been back inside the place once since I phoned you," she said. "I'm used to old houses, but this one gives me the creeps."

We walked towards its old sagging porch. Paint was peeling everywhere.

Bramble led me through an ancient door to an old, musty living room. White sheets covered every piece of furniture. A large, old brass candlestick stood on one side of the dusty mantelpiece. Except for the floor, dust was everywhere.

"Who swept the floor?" I asked.

"Not me. This is exactly how I found the living room," Bramble said. "This is not the kind of house you sell for its cleanliness or the colour of its paint, you know. We call this a DIY special. The right buyer will be looking for the silver lining in this cloud of dust. In fact, the right buyer won't notice the dust at all."

"Why were you here today?" I asked.

"I came over to inspect the house," she said. "I do that with every house, before I show it."

Bramble then proceeded to tell me about her encounter with the ghost. This is more or less how it went:

As Bramble walked through the living room, she began to hear noises. They came from a room near the back of the house. Arming herself with a candlestick, she investigated. She found the door to the room locked. But a key hanging on a nail nearby worked the lock. So she opened the door.

When her eyes adjusted to the darkness, she made out a white figure—or a ghost. "It raised its arms like this," Bramble said, as she flapped her hands at her sides. "And it made an eerie sound."

Bramble was startled, but she didn't think she was in danger. It repeated the same movements over and over. "It looked as if it were trying to frighten me," Bramble said. "Then it lurched forward."

Bramble threw the candlestick at the ghost but missed. She slammed the door and locked it. Then she ran outside and rang me from a call box.

Fifteen minutes later, she re-entered the house. The noises were gone. The door was still locked. The key was still in the lock. When she unlocked the room, she found it empty.

While I had doubts about Bramble's story, I didn't think she was guilty of anything. I took her business card and said I would phone her.

I started my inspection with the lock. It

needed oil, but it worked. It also only worked from the outside. The "ghost" could not have unlocked the door from the inside and escaped.

I inspected the room itself. There was a narrow staircase and the single door that Bramble had opened. The walls were panelled with narrow pieces of dark wood.

The candlestick Bramble had thrown lay on the floor. I looked for a mark on the wall. Sure enough, a large gouge had been taken out of the panelling where the candlestick had hit the wall. I could see the mark from the doorway, where Bramble had been standing when she threw it.

But something was wrong. The candlestick lay off to the side, several strides away from that mark. How could it have landed there? It should have been just below the mark. Its shape made it impossible to roll.

Then I examined the stairs. They led to a loft. They were thick with dust. There were no footprints in the dust. I glanced back around me at the four walls, looking for a window, but there was none.

I took out my sketch pad and made a record of the scene:

As I worked, I wondered if Bramble had made up this strange story. But I couldn't think of a reason why she would lie. The door was locked and there were no footprints on the stairs. How could anyone have disappeared from a locked room without leaving a trace?

As I finished drawing the candlestick in position, I put my pencil down. I decided to try an experiment.

I took the matching candlestick from the mantelpiece in the living room. Then I stood in the doorway, as Bramble said she had done. Taking a good run up, I bowled the heavy candlestick overarm at the wall. It chipped the wood panel, and then fell to the floor where it stopped instantly. It did not roll.

I tried again. And again. And again. After six throws, my candlestick had not once fallen anywhere near the first candlestick.

There was something odd about this whole case. I picked up my pad again, puzzled. I doodled and sketched. The longer I sketched, the more I relaxed. I sat down and leaned back. I closed my eyes.

With my eyes closed, a new image came

to me. For some reason, I imagined the cat burglar who was plaguing the Broadview area. Would he be prowling again tonight? I wondered.

I tore the old sketches off my pad. On a new sheet of paper, I drew the burglar. He carried a large, black bag full of stolen valuables. Where would he take these things?

A successful burglar needs a safe place to hide. Could the Browning house be a hideout? No one lived here. It was also far from the crimes committed. No one would suspect it! If people thought the house was haunted, no one would want to buy it, and people would stay away.

These were all good ideas, but I had no proof. I went back to drawing.

First, I drew the room with the wood panelling. Then I added the candlestick flying through the air and bouncing off the wall. I drew the candlestick again on the floor where it should have landed.

I was definitely onto something. But it didn't answer the questions of the candlestick and the escape from the locked room.

I leaned forward to draw. But this time, when I put my pencil back on paper, the simple answer to both of my questions hit me. Of course! It was the only way.

With a little help from Headquarters, I found my "ghost" within the hour. I had also solved the seven Broadview area burglaries and recovered the stolen property.

I cut up my new drawing and put it in my sketch pad. I had a feeling that when Chief Inspector Anvil worked out this puzzle, he'd see that this was an open-and-shut case.

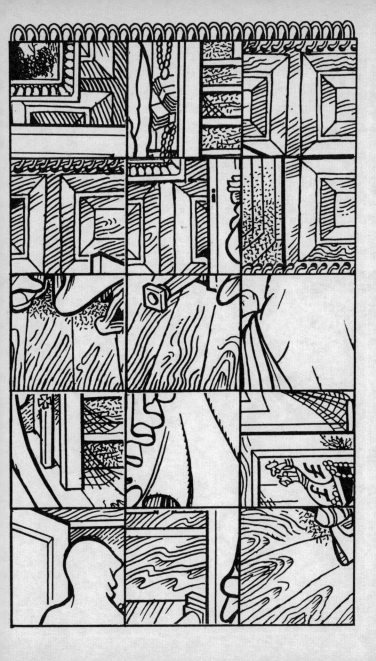

FINAL REPORT

My hunch was right. The Browning house was the burglar's hideout. He used it to store the stolen valuables.

When Bramble threw the candlestick, it bounced off the wall and fell right where it should have. After she locked the door and ran outside, the burglar escaped through a secret door he had discovered in the panelling.

As the hidden door swung open, it pushed the candlestick off to the side. That's exactly where I found it.

—CASE CLOSED—

The Case of the Missing Money

On 19 December, the Managing Director of a big chemical factory in town rang me at Headquarters.

"Detective Riddle, someone has emptied the company safe. All the holiday bonus money for our employees has gone."

I held the phone away from my ear. Robert Gladstone, of the We Care Chemical Company, seemed to enjoy shouting into the receiver.

"I personally checked the safe last night before I left work. It was securely locked. This morning, I unlocked it. It was empty."

I told Gladstone I would be over immediately.

Before I left, I phoned for some help from the fingerprint lab. With any luck, the thief would have left at least one clear fingerprint inside the safe.

Half an hour later, I was on the scene.

The We Care Chemical Company sprawls over thirteen acres of hilly ground at the edge of town. From the main entrance, fields of brightly painted chemical drums and dull grey buildings stretch almost as far as the eye can see.

Robert Gladstone met us inside the main building and led us straight to the safe. It was gigantic. Its shiny round door alone must have weighed 1,000 pounds. The open door was almost big enough to walk through. After a quick look around, I turned the safe over to the fingerprint crew. Gladstone pulled me over to a corner of the room.

"I personally withdrew an enormous amount of cash from our account at the bank yesterday," he boomed. "I put it in the safe myself. It looks as if I was the last honest person to see it."

After a few quick sketches of the safe room, I drove home.

The next morning, fingerprints collected from the We Care Chemical Company safe were on my desk. Two sets of fingerprints were identified: Gladstone's and those of a janitor named Wilbert Fitzwinkle.

I ran a background check on Fitzwinkle, and to my surprise, found that we had a file on him twenty pages long. Among his many crimes were four convictions for safecracking.

That night, we arrested Wilbert Fitzwinkle as he and his wife left the company party. Back at Headquarters I read him the file and he confessed.

But he refused to tell me where he had hidden the money. A week passed. Still he refused.

In desperation, I decided to follow his wife to see if she was suddenly spending a lot of money. Maybe she would lead me to where the money was hidden.

But Betty Fitzwinkle appeared to have no

money. I watched at the bank as she asked for a loan and was turned down.

An envelope from the phone company came to her saying:

A day later, I observed her buying a coat from a second-hand clothes shop.

It was clear she didn't know where the money was.

Finally, the day before the trial, Betty Fitzwinkle gave us a break. While visiting her husband in jail, she begged him for money to buy groceries. The guard assigned to Fitzwinkle overheard their conversation.

"Bring me my grey-striped jacket for the trial tomorrow," Fitzwinkle told her. "And don't forget to sew the torn lining." According to the guard, Fitzwinkle repeated these instructions three times.

Mrs Fitzwinkle finally had to borrow money from the guard. While she headed for the grocers's shop, I drove to the

Fitzwinkles' flat. Why had Fitzwinkle asked his wife three times to sew the lining of his jacket? I suspected that he had hidden something, maybe a map showing where the money was hidden, in the lining of his coat.

I opened the door to the Fitzwinkles' flat with the key that Wilbert Fitzwinkle had turned over to the CID when he was arrested. It took me ten minutes to find the grey-striped jacket hanging in the back of a cupboard in the hall. Sure enough, the lining was torn.

I slipped my hand behind the lining. I found nothing.

Quickly I searched all the pockets. They were empty. I knew there had to be a secret hidden somewhere in the jacket, but I was getting nowhere fast.

Maybe the map wasn't on a piece of paper at all. Maybe it had been written or sewn into the cloth. I turned the jacket inside out and inspected every fold and seam, but I still had no luck.

There was only one thing left to do. Using a pair of Betty Fitzwinkle's sewing scissors, I cut the jacket apart, piece by piece. I pulled out every pocket, every thread. But I still found nothing: no money, no map, no nothing.

Finally, I got up, collected the pieces of the jacket, locked the door, and drove home feeling foolish. It was clear to me now that

Wilbert Fitzwinkle had meant nothing mysterious when he had asked his wife to sew the lining of his jacket.

At home, I made myself some dinner.

But I couldn't eat. My mind was spinning.

I sat down in a chair and took out my drawing pad. I sketched the scene at the Fitzwinkles' apartment—the pieces of the grey-striped jacket lying on the table, Betty Fitzwinkle's sewing basket sitting nearby, full of thimbles, needles, and spools of different-coloured thread. It looked like this:

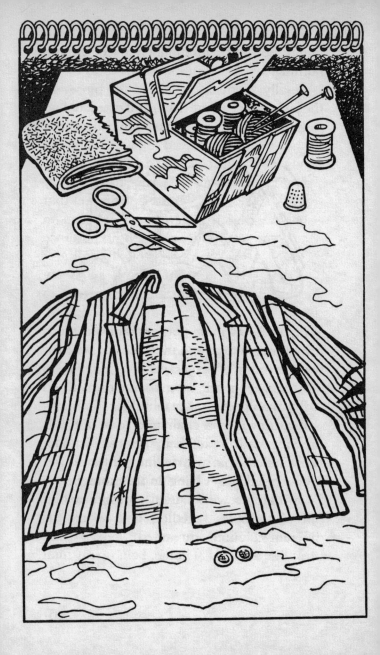

Drawing a picture made me feel calmer, as it always does. But something didn't seem right.

I thought about what Fitzwinkle had been wearing. We had arrested him in a brand-new brown tweed suit with matching trousers. But the jacket he'd asked his wife to bring for the trial was grey-striped. Why would he want to wear a striped jacket that wouldn't match his trousers? I began to think that my first idea about the importance of the jacket was not so far off after all.

I tried to imagine myself in Betty Fitzwinkle's shoes, trying desperately to make sense of her husband's instructions. Fitzwinkle would want to look as smart as possible for the trial. Why then ask for his old, torn jacket? I imagined Betty Fitzwinkle reaching for a needle and thread. I started drawing again.

Suddenly I had it. Simple!

I quickly called Headquarters. "Send an officer to the Fitzwinkle flat right away," I said. "And follow these instructions. . . ."

In less than ten minutes an officer had found the map that showed us where the money was hidden.

While I waited at home, I cut up my final

drawing and put it in the case file on my desk. I could hardly wait to see the look on Chief Inspector Anvil's face when he saw how I'd unravelled this mystery.

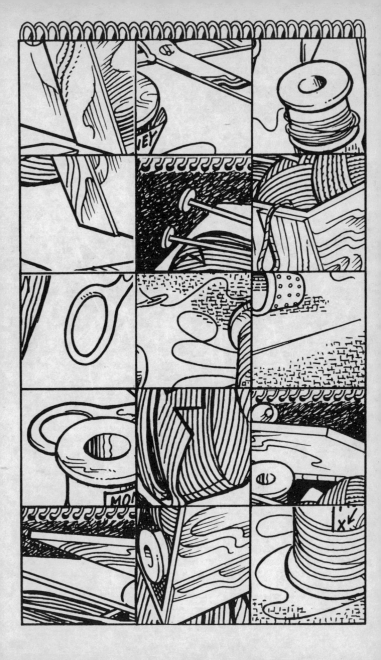

FINAL REPORT

If Betty Fitzwinkle had sewn her husband's jacket, she would have found the hidden map.

Wilbert Fitzwinkle was very clever. He had unwound some grey thread from its spool. Then he wrapped the map around the next layer and rewound the thread over it.

I had handled the grey thread and had never even known I was holding the map that would lead us to Fitzwinkle's stolen money!

—CASE CLOSED—

71

The Case of the Stolen Trees

Just before dark on 22 December, my phone rang at Headquarters.

"Detective Riddle?" said a woman's voice when I answered the phone. "I would like to alert you to a crime in progress in Paisley Park. A man in overalls has parked his blue pickup truck in a corner of the park. He has what looks to be a large handsaw. As we speak, he is cutting down yet another tree. These trees are city property. As a good citizen, I must question this activity. It looks very suspicious."

"I understand," I said.

"Now will you come and arrest him? Or shall I take the law into my own hands?" she asked.

I glanced at my watch. This seemed to be

a case for the Parks Department. But I had planned to have dinner in town anyway.

"I'll be there right away, Miss . . ."

"Mrs Hortensia H Buffington. I live on the sixth floor at the Paisley Manor Hotel, 333 North Avenue."

Ten minutes later, I drove into the circular drive of the Paisley Manor Hotel. As I stopped, a porter opened the back door of my car, and an elderly woman slid into the back seat.

"Turn left there," she said before the porter had closed the car door. "This short cut will bring us directly to the scene of the crime."

We drove into Paisley Park. A minute later she held up her hand and told me to stop.

Our short walk to the scene of the crime took less than a minute. Pine needles were everywhere. About a dozen fresh stumps cut at odd angles rose out of the ground. The smell of pine sap filled the air.

"Those trees had already reached twelve to fifteen feet in height, Detective," said Mrs Buffington. "I remember the day the Friends of Paisley Park planted them—proud Scotch pines, every one. This thief should replace the trees with saplings and tend them until we can no longer tell that any damage occurred. I'd say he deserves at least seven years in the public service."

"Mrs Buffington," I said. "Scotch pines are sold as Christmas trees, are they not?"

"They are the best Christmas trees, in my experience, Detective Riddle. And as you might guess, I have seen more than a few Christmasses."

"Can you describe the man you saw?"

"I saw overalls and a large handsaw, but it was already dark when I called you. He was medium height, I suppose. But I couldn't be certain."

"And the truck?"

She pulled a piece of paper from her handbag. "Here, Detective, is my sketch of the truck. I could not, of course, read the number plate. But with my late husband's binoculars, I could make out the white sign on the side of the truck. It read BETTER CHICKEN FARMS. I'm quite certain of that."

When we returned to the hotel, I called Headquarters. "Tell everyone to look for a blue pickup truck with a white sign on the door," I said.

I thanked Mrs Buffington for her help and good citizenship and promised to let her know when I had solved the case.

That evening, I found the address for Better Chicken Farms in the phone directory. I drove out the next morning. All but one of their pickup trucks were red.

"Yes, sir, we're painting the fleet red," Perkin Peck explained. "We think that it will help people 'think chicken'. You know what I mean? White just didn't do the job. Hard to keep clean, too."

Peck, the owner of Better Chicken Farms, said that he had not owned a blue pickup since 1969. I told him that someone driving a truck with his sign painted on the door had been seen stealing trees.

"No! I can't believe it. This lady who saw it, how good were her eyes?" said Peck.

Back at Headquarters, I found reports on

dozens of blue pickups that had been spotted. But not one had a painted sign. There didn't seem to be a truck in town that matched Mrs Buffington's description.

I decided to drive back to Better Chicken Farms to ask some more questions. Half an hour later, I was back in my car, heading out of town. Suddenly I saw a farm with the sign: CHRISTMAS TREES FOR SALE. ALL SIZES STILL AVAILABLE. I pulled in.

"Selling trees?" I asked.

"Trying to," said the farmer who came out to meet me. "But nobody's buying. Do you want to be the first?" He introduced himself as Herb Flit, "Corn farmer for forty years, tree farmer for ten years, and grandfather for five."

"Do you keep chickens, too?" I asked.

"Chickens? No," Flit said. "You can find chickens in that direction," he said, pointing. "Better Chicken Farms. Just follow your nose."

I looked at the stacks of trees for sale in the snow. They looked tall enough to be from Paisley Park. "Any Scotch pines?" I asked.

"Oh, yes. I have a few fifteen feet tall. Some say Scotch pines are the best. But some don't, so I have Douglas firs, too, but not so tall."

He said he hadn't been to town for weeks.

Then I noticed the blue pickup truck half hidden by a fence near Flit's barn. I asked him if I could have a look.

The truck matched Mrs Buffington's description almost perfectly: a blue pickup with a white sign on the door. The back of the truck was full of pine needles. But the sign on the door did not match Mrs B's description. It read FLIT FARM, not BETTER CHICKEN FARMS. I scratched my ear.

Could Flit have disguised his truck with a Better Chicken Farms sign and then painted over it afterwards? I took a closer look at the sign. I felt each letter carefully with my fingers. Flit had not repainted the sign recently. The fading, pockmarked letters were as old as the truck.

Everything fitted so perfectly—except for the sign. I took out my drawing pad and sketched the truck and sign quickly:

I thanked Flit for his help. On the way out, I counted his Scotch pines.

"Thirteen," said a voice. I spun around. There was no one there.

"Thirteen Christmas trees," said the voice. I looked down. Flit's five-year-old grandson was standing there, drawing numbers on a small blackboard in his hand.

"I can count to thirteen," he said. "Do you want to hear me?" I listened to him twice. Then I showed him how to draw a tree.

Half an hour later, I drove into Paisley Park to count stumps: thirteen again.

How did Flit do it? Suddenly I remembered Christmas. Christmas! If only crime stopped on holidays.

I looked at the scene before me. I was pretty sure that Flit was the thief. Thirteen Scotch pines had been cut down, and he was selling thirteen Scotch pines.

The thief had driven a blue pickup truck with a white sign, and Flit owned a blue pickup with a white sign.

The only thing I couldn't work out was the sign itself. Mrs Buffington said that the thief's truck clearly read BETTER CHICKEN FARMS on the side, but the sign on Flit's truck had not been repainted.

I took out my drawing pad and began to doodle. First I drew the truck again. Then the sign. I continued to draw.

I found myself wondering what Flit would give his grandchild for Christmas. Maybe a toy pickup truck. The kid seemed to have artistic talent, too. Maybe Flit would give him a new chalk set or . . .

Suddenly I had it. I looked at my drawing. Could it be?

I drove to Paisley Manor Hotel and phoned Headquarters. I also left a quick note for Mrs Buffington as I'd promised. Then I headed out to Flit Farm to arrest Herb Flit. I remembered Mrs Buffington's suggestion for punishing the tree thief. I felt the punishment fitted the crime.

When I got home that night I cut up my last drawing and placed it in the file. When Chief Inspector Anvil put this puzzle together, I knew he'd see that I had filled in all the details.

FINAL REPORT

I really should thank Flit's five-year-old grandson for helping me solve this one.

Now I know why Flit's sign was as old as his truck. He didn't paint *over* it. He *added to* it!

Flit had added chalk lines to the letters of FLIT FARM. The sign became BETTER CHICKEN FARMS.

After he stole the trees, Flit erased the evidence.

—CASE CLOSED—

The Case of the
Morning Monsters

Early one Friday morning, an elderly neighbour of mine rang me up. As I picked up the phone the sun was just breaking through the fog.

"Alexander, this is Peter Ploop. We're scared out of our wits today. Chester, Maggie, and I went to rescue a kitten and came face-to-face with a monster. We need your help."

I struggled not to laugh. Peter Ploop, Chester Fester, and Maggie Clickbeetle had been out of their minds for at least seventy years. This had nothing to do with age. They'd been crazy even when they'd met each other at primary school. They were still best friends after all these years.

"The poor kitten," Peter continued. "Her careless master shut her up in a shed. Can you imagine?

"But when we tried to save her, we couldn't get near her. She's guarded by a monster! You must come and help us at once. We'll meet you at Maggie's."

My experience with these three told me not to ignore their strange request. Peter, Chester, and Maggie had already caused more than their fair share of neighbourhood mischief this spring. I put on a sweater and grabbed my pad.

"Sit down," Maggie said when I arrived, offering me a pink rocking chair. As usual, she was a sight in her long black cape. Her

hairdo looked like a big tornado turned upside-down. I couldn't decide if she looked more like the bride of Frankenstein or a woman with a beehive on her head.

"I have an hour," I said.

"Now what's the rush, Alexander?" said Peter. Peter Ploop had once been a college professor. No matter what the weather, Peter always dressed in a tweed jacket. He had a pointy pipe in his mouth, even though he didn't smoke. And because he thought it made him look distinguished, Peter carried a walking stick.

"We walked together early this morning," Maggie began, "as we do every morning. But today, we heard a kitten mewing loudly somewhere in the fog. The pitiful sound seemed to be coming from the new house on the corner. It has a fence around it. Do you know it?"

I nodded.

"I simply could not walk past without trying to help," Maggie continued. "So I asked my two friends here to wait for me. And then I marched straight into the garden to do my good deed."

There were piles of wood everywhere," added Peter. "She could have tripped in the fog. She shouldn't have gone.''

"But I did," said Maggie, glaring. "The sounds were coming from a large tool shed."

"She saw a monster!" Chester burst in.

"I did not," Maggie said, stamping her foot. "There was very little light inside the shed, but I could just make out the shapes of tools, boards, a large piece of equipment covered with a cloth, a kitten—and hovering over it, the outline of a monstrous bird. It had huge dark wings and a pointed head! As I moved towards the kitten to rescue it, the bird spread its wings."

"She saw a monster!" Chester said again, slapping the knee patches on his baggy trousers.

Of the three, Chester dressed the most plainly—but his clothes always looked four sizes too big. Today, he had rolled the sleeves of his trench coat above his elbows and turned the collar up. The long points of this overstarched coat collar looked like two soldiers standing to attention on opposite sides of a steep hill.

Chester continued, "Maggie wouldn't change her story, so Peter offered to go and rescue the kitten. But he came back as white as a sheet!"

"The kitten was there, all right," Peter began. "I saw the tools, the cloth and everything. But I saw nothing like a bird. The strange creature that I saw had the head of a rhinoceros. I saw its outline very clearly. But only its head was animal! As I raised my arm to protect myself, it pointed a stick at me. Then it attacked me."

"So it was Chester's turn to rescue the kitten," Maggie said.

"I didn't believe a word these two said, Alexander. Really I didn't," Chester began. "I thought they had turned one of our little pranks on its head. But no! I saw the kitten, yes, and a cloth and some tools. But no bird or rhino. The outline I saw had two sharp horns—like a bull! It moved, but not in a threatening way. I myself am not afraid of bulls, so I was perfectly relaxed."

"Chester was so 'relaxed', he ran straight

past us," Maggie added, laughing. "And he didn't stop running until he got back here."

"Shall we visit the shed now?" I asked.

"If we must," Maggie said, disappointed. "We were hoping you would work out the truth from our stories just by us telling you them."

"A good detective must trust his own eyes," Peter said.

"No," I said, changing my mind. "No, I'll accept your challenge. I will solve this strange case without visiting the scene. But you three have to promise me one thing."

"Name it," said Peter.

"Promise to give up your pranks for the summer," I said firmly.

"No pranks?" cried Maggie. "Oh, dear."

"I think that's fair," said Peter.

"But you must also free the kitten," Chester added somewhat anxiously.

"I will free the kitten. But I must draw a while. Can the kitten survive fifteen minutes more?"

Maggie nodded thoughtfully.

I moved to Maggie's porch so I could be alone. I took out my drawing pad. I sketched my troublesome trio, just as they had appeared before me:

Then I sat back and thought about the stories I had just heard.

First, each witness had seen the kitten, so their stories agreed on at least one point. Next, everyone had seen tools and something covered with a cloth.

That gave me an idea. Could the equipment under the cloth have looked like a monster? No. All three said they had seen the monster move. But wait! Had everyone seen the creature clearly? No, they hadn't! In fact, one saw a bird, one saw a rhino, and one saw a bull. And hadn't they said it was foggy outside and very little light had entered the shed? Everyone had used the word "outline". Not one of them had seen the monster in any great detail.

I thought some more. I imagined my neighbours coming face-to-face with their monster. . . .

Then I began a new drawing. It was of Maggie Clickbeetle being attacked by a monster bird. Suddenly I saw it clearly. I had the solution!

I cut up my drawing and put it in my sketch pad. When Chief Inspector Anvil looked into this puzzle, and paused to reflect on how I'd solved this case, he'd know that I had been a good detective.

After slipping a quick note under Maggie's front door, I headed off to rescue the stray kitten. I thought I just might keep it.

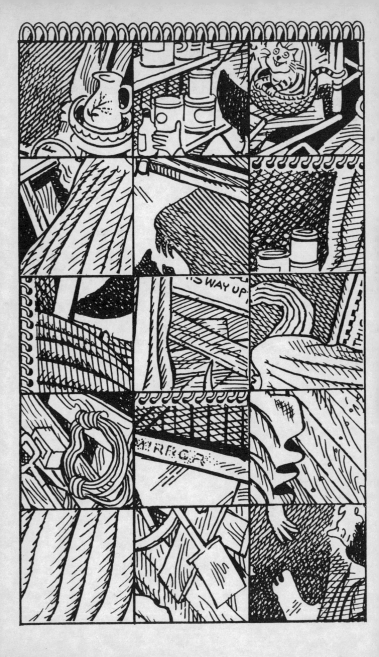

FINAL REPORT

I drew a picture of Maggie Clickbeetle coming face-to-face with a monstrous bird. Suddenly I knew there could be only one solution.

There was a big mirror inside the darkened toolshed!

Maggie had been looking at an outline of *herself.* The bird's pointed head was Maggie's funny hairdo. And its wings were her long cape.

Chester had never seen a sharp-horned bull. It was the points of his coat collar that stuck out on each side of his head.

And as for Peter, the pointy pipe in his mouth made his reflection look exactly like a rhinoceros. Peter was embarrassed when I told him that he had attacked himself with his own cane.

—CASE CLOSED—

More great puzzle books from Hippo:

Mindbenders *Deborah Manley*
If you enjoy fiddling with figures, worrying about words and lingering over letters, *Mindbenders* is the puzzle book for you. With over 500 questions, games, tricks and conundrums, it's guaranteed to leave those brain cells tied up in knots! £1.95

The Nature Puzzle Book *Ron Wilson*
From ants to elephants, whelks to whales and poppies to poplar trees . . . this book will stretch your knowledge of the natural world. But with riddles, a crossword, anagrams and word squares, finding the answers is terrific fun! £1.95

You Be the Jury *Marvin Miller*
The court is in session, the trial is set to begin, and YOU are the jury . . .
Ten intriguing courtroom mysteries are played out before you. You examine each case, study the evidence, then make your decision! Can you puzzle out the answers from the evidence given? £1.75

You Be the Jury 2 *Marvin Miller*
Twenty more courtroom mysteries for you to examine and work out the verdict. £1.75